January 1, 1986

And another great year to you...

Love,

Gene Hoyt

Life
Among
Others

By Daniel Halpern

Poetry

LIFE AMONG OTHERS

STREET FIRE

THE LADY KNIFE-THROWER

TRAVELING ON CREDIT

Translator

THE SONGS OF MRIRIDA

Editor

THE AMERICAN POETRY ANTHOLOGY

BORGES ON WRITING

(with Norman Thomas di Giovanni and Frank MacShane)

Daniel Halpern

Life Among Others

THE VIKING PRESS
NEW YORK

First published in 1978 by The Viking Press
625 Madison Avenue, New York, N.Y. 10022
Published simultaneously in Canada by
Penguin Books Canada Limited

LIBRARY OF CONGRESS CATALOGING IN PUBLICATION DATA
Halpern, Daniel, 1945–
Life among others.
I. Title.
PS3558.A397L5   1978b   811'.5'4   77–25925
ISBN 0-670–42788–8

Printed in the United States of America
Set in Linotype Bodoni Book

ACKNOWLEDGMENT:
Alfred A. Knopf, Inc. From
"Final Soliloquy of the Interior Paramour"
from *The Collected Poems of Wallace Stevens.*
Copyright 1951 by Wallace Stevens.
Reprinted by permission.

SOME OF THESE POEMS HAVE APPEARED IN
THE FOLLOWING PERIODICALS:
American Poetry Review: "In My House of Others," "Summer House"; *American Review:* "I Am a Dancer"; *Antioch Review:* "Fish"; *Atlantic Monthly:* "Aubade," "I Hear Nothing"; *Georgia Review:* "The Hero at Midnight," "Above the Port"; *Harper's Magazine:* "Take for Example," "Blue Suspension"; *The Iowa Review:* "For You," "Lime Kiln," "Distant Faces," "Person Smoking"; *The Nation:* "Let Me Tell You"; *New Republic:* "Letter to the Midwest"; *The New Yorker:* "Still"; *North American Review:* "Letter to the Midwest," "Family Likeness"; *Paris Review:* "Clams"; *Ploughshares:* "Landmarks"; *Poetry Northwest:* "What Matters Is the Room Itself"; *Poetry Now:* "Distance," "Suspension," "Sunset Tattoo"; *Prairie Schooner:* "Sad Ending"; *Salmagundi:* "White Tent," "White Train," "White Contact"; *Southern Review:* "Long Distance"; *Virginia Quarterly Review:* "The Dance."

Out of this same light, out of the central mind,
We make a dwelling in the evening air,
In which being there together is enough.

—WALLACE STEVENS

CONTENTS

I

II

I

My solitude grew more and more obese,
like a pig.

—YUKIO MISHIMA

You do not need to leave your room. Remain sitting
at your table and listen. Do not even listen, simply
wait. Do not even wait, be quite still and solitary. The
world will freely offer itself to you to be unmasked,
it has no choice, it will roll in ecstasy at your feet.

—FRANZ KAFKA

TAKE FOR EXAMPLE

Take the insect for example.
The pale wings that work in air
and the singing legs.

It goes forth into the air
unafraid. It can return
to the place it set out from,

or it can continue flying, outward.
If it does not turn back
it is always singing

to some new part of the world
as it passes—to the flower
in its first opening,

to the leaf floating on a branch,
to the bird upon the grass,
to the window and the house,

to the man who slaps the song
between his hands
in the one applause he knows.

And the man goes back.
He goes back to the place
he set out from without a song.

IN MY HOUSE OF OTHERS

I take the hand of others.
With this gesture I do not
stay away: if I walk into the street
(the sun not too bright, the people
not too numerous), it is the hand
of others that takes me—
past the bright places,
past the insects that do not harm
with their erratic movement,
past the small and large houses of others
that line the road out of town,
away from the room where I live
in a list. This is the life
that feels too little outside itself,
this is the life that inflates
the dream of taking away
that goes with me down the street
and is with me in the night
when the voices of what I must recall
answer back, and in time
hold me.

LIFE AMONG OTHERS

I tempt light off the bay till evening
moves across the hills and presses
into the city its engraver's ink. I won't say
why I'm here, or why I remain without moving
by day into the night. At the hotel
the lights in the other rooms go on one by one,
and in the garden, which overlooks the markets
of the old city, the palms flap, rooted
birds with green tropical wings.
The guests are at tangerines and Vichy
before the evening meal. While they eat
I sit in front of my window, I tempt
the solitary lights that go on and off
on the water: lights of boats, cape lights,
the lights across the water. They pile up
in darkness here. It is a collection, a pastime.
Now I have the chance to speak—not to explain
but to return everything—your bright lives
rooted to nothing more than a light seen at a distance
that diminishes as it moves closer and closer.
Where I am there is everything that is beautiful.
It is where I started out,
it is where I think of you now.
From this setting of props, I return it all.

THE MOLE

Outside another cheery day is going on.
The gay life in the sun that breeds
the darkness that lasts into night.
I live outside in the continuously cheery day—
the brides are white, the air is white,
the dresses of the children are white.
I walk among so much, and touch the skin
or eyes of those in light. The days last
as long as they can, and the darkness
grows from behind the trees and houses.
So what good is so much cheer? Outside the dark
streets end in more darkness. Somewhere children
are in bright rooms with their parents.
It is night, and as I enter sleep
the last movements are going on.
This is the other part, the mole
soundless, sliding beneath me—its dark life
only movement, constant night, something long and steady,
unchanging except for the cool and the warm turning
over and over till I wake.

ABOVE THE PORT

The room you've built night after night
is finally yours.
You sit on the bed, you lie down,
you watch the moiré patterns of the white gauze
curtains float in and out the window.
This is what you've wanted for so long:
the sea wind, the afternoon sleep,
the fish and wine and heavy dark bread.
You fall asleep, and in sleep
the old rooms return with friends,
and you are among them. When you wake
you are lonely, and yet
you have everything: the clean white room
above the port, the curtains, the fish.
Still, it is all just a little sad.
You look out and see the light at Malabata,
the lights across the Straits in Spain.
The room is dark, and you've already slept.

YOU GO OUT

You don't always feel well,
you'll want to lie down,
press your face
against the cool cement floor.
You'll want to go out,
leave behind what order
you've managed these years.

You go out into the street.
The fires there go out
and the faint glow at the bottom
of the sky moves up and blossoms.

You feel well in the company of others,
neighbors and pets, trash
in the smoking bonfires.
You are no longer the stranger
who made too little sense.

One day you go out,
you get up from the cement floor
and you go out.
It is time to say everything,
to give up order and move on.

LANDMARKS

Don't turn around.
It is the expected
behind us. We have only
to move forward
along the stalk of surprise
as it grows and branches.

It is winter. The trees
march away from the window
like the ghostly skeletons of fish.
They take me from this place,
stalks that lead to the next season,
landmarks that become the road away.

DISTANCE

These are the wares of leaving,
implements of guidance that ask
nothing more than to take you
farther away. Their bodies
seem at first like fires
burning until they become cool beacons
from a place that is dark.
By your eyes, this is the way you go.

These are the wares of arrival,
implements of seduction that ask
nothing more than to bring you
all the way to them. They are lights
or bodies of heat burning
in a place that is dark
until they begin to burn for you,
show the way home. You leave
by light, and by light you arrive.
You reach the door that was once distant
and look back.
Again, in the distance, a light begins to burn.

WHAT MATTERS IS
THE ROOM ITSELF

I entered the room where they slept
and they were awake.
I said I was leaving.
They talked among themselves
and though they saw I was there
they said nothing to me.
I entered the room to talk with them,
to explain how we shared
the pale light of day,
the blood light of early evening,
to say good-bye to them.
From their beds they spoke only to each other.

This is the room where I rest now.
They are gone,
or they have never been here.
The light is pale,
or it has the cast of blood
as it breaks over the trees.
Who they were and why they were here
comes back to me—they were awake
and although they said nothing to me
they spoke among themselves.
They kept me with them
and I am here now

as another enters the room.
She speaks to me and receives no answer.
I see her in the light.
She tells me she is leaving,
but she will enter this room
where what we say means nothing,
like the light, like the day
and the early evening that light the room.

PERSON SMOKING

Cigarette smoke floats up
to this second-story room.
It doesn't mean too much,
but it is a sensation.
Below me someone sits quietly.
There is no reason to believe
it is a woman, and there is no way
I can look out the window.
I imagine a woman sitting on a bench
smoking quietly, looking off
into the trees. I could of course
call out, but that would be ridiculous.
I wonder, as I stare into the trees,
what she is thinking about.
She can't know I'm here
and wouldn't care if she did.
She sits there as I sit here.
And then she laughs.
Startled, I turn back
into the room. She watches me
from the bed, smiling gently—
at what, I wonder.
Her cigarette is a gray ash that drops
into the white air of the sheets.

DISTANT FACES

Sometimes at night
I go out to the terrace
lit by red neon
that vibrates the still air.
I lie down on bricks
whose coolness calms me
and remember those who have left
for cities in the west,
or the midwest,
or for nowhere at all.
After a little I go back in,
and in sleep call back
those familiar faces.
Or else I remain on the bricks
and press to my body
the coolness that keeps
those who have left me
so distant, so far away.

GLASSWORKS

You run out of invention and the glass stem
that holds the object snaps.
Nearly complete, the object rolls away
with the truth of completion still unformed.
What a sad life that uses the body
like this, to support what lives above it,
and make it live below intelligence.

LIME KILN

Late August, the dead days of lime
　　bleaching clay near the kiln
　　　　at Big Sur. I move forward

in shoes bleached by lime and sun,
　　and in my face the stain
　　　　of lime moving upon me.

The dead pots hump in corners
　　around the shack. No music here
　　　　but the music of white bone

drying beyond water in sun.
　　Late August. I bring back distant
　　　　summers—the air of memory,

the distal air of avatars
　　mixing water and mud, clay,
　　　　the admixture of sky and earth.

A few miles away the sea wind
　　moves, sweeps salt in sheets over birds.
　　　　I sit now on the gray wood

of the kiln's benches. It is bright.
   The salt, like birds hovering,
      moves on. I have never been here.

I'll leave no bones still pink with flesh
   or blood. There are no bones to leave.
      There are no thoughts to leave. Only

the mind runneled like earth, dry
   and bare as the limed earth,
      nothing but the wet flesh of memory.

THE HERO AT MIDNIGHT

One begins with an open mouth,
with everything.
Food comes your way,
movement,
inescapable romance,
inescapable choice.
You learn to take what you can.

But this isn't the way
you wanted it,
that simple, so much
for yourself.
It is not, as you look back,
that life was so complex:

remember the bright green
head of the mallard
you tamed the year you were eight,
the beach at night on blankets,
watching the surf
pen a thin white line
down the beach.

Now in your room you can think
about it all—

maybe you have everything,
maybe not enough.
In the trees outside
birds still wet with birth
peep for food and get it.
The moth at night comes
out of darkness for light,
and gets it.

I sit on the edge of the bed
and think about this.
Already it's too late to say
the few things
I'd hoped to say alone.

BEGIN

We are in the room.
The light, the lizards on the screen
and the overhead fan are givens.
Now as we sit the light is going out.
Have you come to take what I say
to others? I say little:
the air that fills speech lies
in its chamber.
Light the candles—we will sit up tonight.
If you are quiet I will tell you.
I need only begin. Can you hear me?

SUSPENSION

I don't say it
We sit together
It becomes the thing not said
It's not that I want to keep it from you
It comes forward in dream
And steps back into itself in light
How can I bring it to you
How can I hold it myself out of sleep
This is not the way I wanted it
To hold back everything
You listen
It seems like nothing
My hands floating without body
My body turning in air
I pretend to sleep
Let me tell you what it is
Let me tell you what it is

SUNSET TATTOO

for D. Schmitz

There are no sunsets here,
sunsets are endings.
Only muted sun
and the shadows of buildings
that keep the temperature too low,
and in the streets
fires burning without heat.

I need a thousand details
to keep going—
they are what I know
of myself among others.
I am held upright
but can't let myself go:
a symptom, but minor.
Another minor detail
to carry around
like a dollar bill.

There is only the sun rising—
every day the same
over the same details
of earth
at exactly the right moment—
rising.

STILL

I hear callers in the trees,
but I stay in one place,
knowing motion is nothing
if I can't stand like this
hour after hour.

In this immobility a fire inflates,
and so much turbulence within the static—
the owls call, still in their trees.
They can see in the night, they don't need to move.
I don't move myself—the river moves

somewhere, the clouds without sound
move and move. They drift and disband.
The dogs are still, except for their jaws,
which click in the night.
They smell the darkness, they don't need to move.

My work is to stand still and see everything.
My work is to rethink the immobile,
the owl and dog, and without moving release them,
release myself, let everything live again,
recalled into movement and loved, wholly still.

II

At evening the hermits see the lights come on at the windows; the wind bears, in gusts, the music of festivities. In a quarter of an hour, if they chose, they could be back among other people. The hermit's strength is measured not by how far away he has gone to live, but by the scant distance he requires to detach himself from the city, without ever losing sight of it.

—ITALO CALVINO

AUBADE

We take off our clothes
and enter the dark.
We are each unlike any other.
The weather doesn't matter,
our indifferent touching doesn't matter.
Not even the cloth of darkness
in a foreign room can make it different.
The hand in its least movement is a difference.
The body in its turning is a difference.
It is when I fall to dream in your arms
that I climb into the arms of another:
her fingers like no others; we turn
into the dark, deeper, deeper,
the black cloth unraveling
until I am back again beside you
in the first light, the morning of the different day.

FOR YOU

You are not going to say any more now—
we are in bed and your fingers are closed
between your legs.
My hands are in their chambers.
We are talking with a low-watt bulb burning.
It is not sordid. It is raining.
There is unfriendliness between us
and your long white men's flannels.
For too long there has been cloth
between us.
                    Later the cat
will move down your length, a warm ball of fur
between us. My 800-pound arm
is sex, all man between us.
It is late. It is raining.
Others have conspired in this taking apart.
Objects have kept us
from each other.
In the front room there is an Eve all male.
The feeling here for you is all mine
and you are lost,
powerful, unsure—your angry renegade head. . . .

You are not sure.
I will find you
again and again.
You have held yourself against me.
You say,
This last long river is for you.

LETTER TO THE MIDWEST

for Louise

You would notice the humor: storks
at work in the fields collecting seeds,
the pointing tips of *djellabas*
that stick up at odd angles—
closer to God, perhaps. The palms are dramatic,
waving wildly in wind. At their centers
the rust-colored fronds remain still.
You, of course, see the irony in this.
The rain stops and starts all day,
the horns left over from the Europeans'
New Year still sound in every street.
It's exotic all right.
It makes me gloomy and I imagine
snow fields without storks, corn instead of *kif*,
and little children off to school,
their hair lighter than snow,
speaking English, their mothers' kisses
still blossoming on their rosy cheeks.
But it's dusk here,
veiled figures go by outside my window,
the lights across the Straits begin to appear.
The bats have begun to feed, and the starlings,
in a frenzy, circle, and float home.

LONG DISTANCE

*Back of the world in which we live, far in the background, lies
another world.... Many people who appear bodily in the actual
world do not belong in it but in that other. But the fact that a
man can thus dwindle away, aye, almost vanish from reality, may
be a symptom of health or of sickness.*

—SØREN KIERKEGAARD

I am disguised in the world you make for yourself
walking with a postcard or phone call,
your scaling boots strong as roots, and rain
too thick for others to move through, outside your window
after you've come through that rain. Hot water
stalls in your hair, moves down.
I feel what I don't know,
your voice through the midwest, the lines that move
pole after pole three times a thousand miles
to reach me in the moment of speech. There are drunks
in Nebraska—there is still Kansas—who hear
only the buzz of our lives together in the distance
of time ahead, the hum of wires and country people
lined into Illinois and then New York,
the East, the sober breath
of the Atlantic that keeps me from leaning home.
Your voice stays steady on the wire that brings you.

I have your photograph before me:
your arm raised with little sign of breast

31

and your hair moving past your hips—your
strong face smiling somewhere in my disguise,
in the woods where you walk with me at times, at times
thinking of the rough bark telling you
of life beneath oak and dark undergrowth
of what seems unseen. That darkness.
We get to this with a slowness that amazes—
the night, when the light moves off and your hands,
ungummed, take on the lineaments of personality.
As the repulsive grows a root in the heart-eye kept silent,
the frail fern lives in the wet under-earth
of tree shadow in your first moments here,
for the beginning when the door you've yet to touch
opens. You won't see me:
you'll find the hall over my shoulder opening
onto music selected for this, the scent
from a wooden box of oils moving out for you
in clear smoke, bringing you in.

THE DANCE

No one's dancing here tonight.
Wouldn't you know it.
The cat in profile smiles at the light,
the rain is just a little sound on the metal
of the roof—out of season.

The cat doesn't dance and I wouldn't watch
if she did. Her little soul though
dances tonight, she is so pleased we are alone.
She smells the roast in the kitchen
and for my sake appreciates its progress.

There is a little fire burning: sawdust pressed
into a log and sold for a dollar keeps the light
the right tone and the heat up, although
it isn't really cold. No one is dancing,
the candles have been punched out,

and the amber has worn off the hardwood box.
Even the music, if it were playing, would make it
no different. Not even the rain or the food.
It doesn't matter little friend.
No one's dancing here tonight—wouldn't you know it.

I HEAR NOTHING

I hear nothing, you always hear the rain.
What deep sleep I fall into. But explain
what holds you in bed and keeps you awake

night after night. Is it for my sake
you say nothing when I open my eyes
and catch you looking into air? What lies

in the house of your vigil? You talk
only of night sounds, of the last to walk
home, the sound of their alcoholic steps.

I ask for what you hear beyond footsteps,
something you are unable to explain.
I hear nothing. You always hear the rain.

SAD ENDINGS

after Bashō

Years ago I would have written,
"This is the way it is for those like us."
And you would have replied,
"My dear, I thank you for your frankness. You
were always too kind to me. Now, I must take my leave."

    Sweetheart, I'm old-fashioned. My heart
is no longer plump fruit. I walk in
to hold you, and you are not there.
At night, I sleep only to hold you
in dream, a few seconds perhaps;
and I wake, but I wake without your scent.
It is all dream. You live in another city
with other people. I am only the young man
you loaned your smile to for a while.

    How sentimental you are, sweet man, to write
me in this way. Of course I value everything—
how full of humor you were in the morning
with the other women—I remember especially
your clever white hands articulating the word,
your feet turned in like a dancer's, but flat.
If I smiled I smiled with pleasure. But let us
be friends, and I shall come to your city for visits,
for meals, if you'll make them, for conversation
between friends. How sweet of you to think of me.
If time allows, please write again. Fondly,

And how simple it all is. Someone finally just walks
away. It might be sunset, but it mustn't be.
The one who leaves is moved
less than the left,
but both are touched, and touched in different ways.
One leaves, one remains:
For you who go, for me who stays, two autumns.

BLUE SUSPENSION

Brown wood and moss-covering,
women, their wicker baskets

of dark bread and cold meats, wine
and the girl who wore the denim dress,

whose eyes I never saw in the strange
light of the afternoon. Take this

photograph from me, the lawn filled
with mallets and colored balls, wickets

and the trimmed hedge. I remember this,
the summer and the summer baskets, her dress

and the water when I found her, the strange
light on wood below the surface of water,

the dress fluttering there, fluttering
as if in a wind, as if I were seeing it

from the lawn, a dark wood scent still upon me,
the dry feel of the wooden mallet in my hands,

the bright balls moving toward wickets, the black
bread, the red wine, the girl in her blue suspension.

FISH

She is washed by white-water, white if she looked up.
She fingers the pebbles. This fancy of water for her,
touched now only by surf
and the gray temples of kelp.
There is a single boy in a caïque,
his drop line and the fish that moves off,
hooked, thinking itself free
with the taste of silver. The fish
is not destined to return with flesh of the hunt.
It moves for the woman on the beach without reason.
Its smooth body takes on the legs of the boy
in shallow water, grows a face
and stands in air, breathing
as if for the first time, and walks
to where the woman waits.
As the boy in the boat begins to sink
the fish touches the woman
on her hair that spreads upon her shoulders.
The kelp is green in the shallows beyond the breakers
where the boy descends—
the fish now tall in the light, the woman's hair, yellow
from the cliffs over her shoulders.
The boy descending. The woman looking up.
The fish bending to touch her.

CLAMS

The gift of clams is here, waiting
in the large bowl on the cutting table.
We are waiting: the clams
softly opening and closing.
I am in the kitchen, organizing
our hundred bottles of spice.
I take down oregano and sweet basil,
grate the cheese you forgot to cover,
and continue waiting.
The clams wait in their bowl.
They continue opening and closing—
closing when they think
I am looking at them. They are waiting
for the knife that will bare them to the world,
where they will taste the spices of the shelf,
giving up their grip on life.
I am waiting with this gift of clams.
In their opening and closing
they try to tell me something
of the hollow between their shells.
Or is it not to pry
into things I won't in the end understand?—
this gentle conversation in released sea air,
this gift of clams.

LET ME TELL YOU

What is it that is missed: the time
as it slides through familiar light?
the cat, a dark rock under the light?
I can think of nothing to say to you.

The red brick of the walls outside my room
grows softer as the days pass. The fly
on the curtain grows fat. One day
it will grow too fat, too lonely.

I think back to another place I left
long ago: mock tropical, too warm
to live in. Distance couldn't transform
it—it was that far away.

But that is farther away
than what is missed now,
and you have nothing to say.
People pair up against the lonely

like me. How can I write you of this?
Each morning the couples come down—
they bring what they would miss,
they can eat together. It is all gesture

in the end—to leave what you need
behind, to bring it with you. It is
all the same. How difficult
it is to tell you what I need.

FAMILY LIKENESS

This is not my father's room.
He has not been here in his silence,
and I have not asked him.
Nor was I ever his guest.

In one corner of this room the light
is on the table where dill grows in a box.
I use it for salad, or eggs, or veal
in its pale sauce. The salad is of red

lettuce; but it is not for the food
that I discuss the room. There is a mirror
I stand in front of and speak to myself
as I speak now, after years, to others.

I take off my clothes and place my hands
on the layers of fat that have collected.
This is how the food becomes part of the room,
and why my father is for the moment with me here.

As I stand before the mirror it is the fat
that calls back to him this last time:
not as guest or friend or likeness,
but as one too thin from giving up so little.

PHOTOGRAPH

I. D. H. 1921–1970

I've never felt this way before, he said,
his last words, so the nurse said.
I went behind the curtain and touched his hand.
I thought of the drunk woman
who jumped into my car
as I waited for my parents
outside the restaurant the day we learned
of my father's illness. She lifted her dress
and said, *Want to feel something
you've never felt before?* I thought of my father
putting his arms around me, needing me
to carry him to the car.
I remember his pale eyes looking at me.
I took the last picture of him:
he stood in the driveway of our house
on Chandler Boulevard in a white T-shirt,
looking back at the camera. The smoke
of the cigar he held in his right hand
turned back against his thin wrist.
The curtain in the room was brown,
his hand, still warm, felt nothing.

SUMMER HOUSE

for Mark

There is a house
that overlooks St. Margaret's Bay.
You lived there as a child
with your aunt and mother.
Looking back now you think of Albert,
the fisherman with one leg.
He took you out in his dory
before sunrise, out to where the nets
were thrown and drawn in
boiling with mackerel and herring.
Evenings you went down to the landing
to pitchfork skate.
You guess the house now is almost gone,
the walls dried out, punched in
and scattered by the salt wind.
It is a house you would buy if you could,
but what it held for you is gone;
what we know of it is in your face
as you tell us the story of your summers
and your father's occasional visits.
What is left is no longer the house,
or Albert, or the women cooking fish
in the heat of late afternoon.
Of those summers still lingering
you see only your father
with unmistakable clarity,
reading in the front room, by lamplight.

WHITE TENT

I pitched a tent in an open field
near what you thought were white birds
searching for seeds in an open field.
They were white tents pitched
here and there, and inside each a fire
burned with a single voice.
I built myself out of these white tents:
it doesn't matter what each voice said,
that I was many things—a stick
beating a sad dog, a woman standing
in any empty house, looking away,
a young boy running in place on a beach.
In my tent I pieced something together
and went back out into the field,
clothed in these many voices. The tents
turned back to white birds. White birds
took flight, lifted off the ground
their ultimate kindness and watched me
grow smaller and smaller, a hornet
without wings, walking back to the road
where you waited, looking after the birds
as they lifted, and disappeared.

WHITE TRAIN

The night knows nothing of the chants of night
calling within it—songs that tremble
vibrato in blue air: Datura,
scent of your body that shakes itself from you
and becomes what the night never knows.
It is no dream that the white train shunts
within the chant of night.
The white voice of the muezzin, gentle
in its response, is no dream.
I know nothing more than scent,
the sense of touch where nothing sees.
I touch you
and it doesn't matter that the night
knows nothing.
Datura—white bell of the garden,
scent of the dead—does the muezzin
lie in his song? Is the white train
not going to return?
The night doesn't answer. It touches everything
and hears nothing. I touch you like this.
This is no dream. I know nothing.

WHITE CONTACT

There is a boy running along the beach.
But he is a boy only
if seen at a distance.
He is the man who left a house,
the woman who lived there,
and the white contact between them.
White, the color of clarity
where nothing has to live.
It matches everything and can go
anywhere. It fits in and is nothing.
White contact in a house where nothing
is said. Does he need to hurt her
in any other way? He cannot tell you.
She stands alone in the house
in the same way as when he was there.
It does not matter to her that he is gone,
or that he is running now toward something
far ahead that will remain small.
He rebukes her as he runs, he forgets her,
there is more and more to forget—
no contact, he thinks, only his feet
on the sand, smaller and smaller—leaving
behind the house, her hand—to become the boy,
running along the beach.

I AM A DANCER

There is no reason to be bothered,
to bother. Once you begin the anger
there is no telling where it will end.
But I sit down now and begin.
Is this the anger that takes up the stick?
The anger that is a silence in silence?
The thing not done, or done too late?
What a quiet little man I seem,
alone in a room with four walls
and, these days, something
of interest to make the days more interesting.
What is it the others want? Like?
They don't know. Do I miss them?
Let the dream take over now—white
train, white bird, white tent—white images
that lift away. This is how I work.
Myself, I am a dancer, feinting, refusing
to be there for you. It is not
that I don't care. The tent of dream
is a privacy, the bird a way out,
the train, power to keep on. I'm not
really unpleasant, and there is no crime
committed against others. Myself. No
madness, no crazy man behind bars. I
am the inmate. The crime

is only a little fear. I begin now
to beat it. To piece back together
the destruction of the walls.
I kick open the air and, my friend, I walk out.